CHIP

JESSIE

Written and drawn by
Shirley Hughes

Fontana Young Lions

For Paul Edward

First published in Great Britain 1985 by The Bodley Head Ltd
First published in Fontana Young Lions 1987
8 Grafton Street, London W1X 3LA

Fontana Young Lions is an imprint of
Fontana Paperbacks, part of
the Collins Publishing Group

Printed in Great Britain
by William Collins Sons & Co. Ltd, Glasgow

Do hurry up and get on with it!

O.K., O.K., Hello, everyone!

I'm Chips and she's Jessie and this is our book. I mean, Shirley Hughes wrote it, but we're the main people in it. And this is the introduction, which I wrote myself (well, Jessie helped a bit).

Dear All,

Jessie and I thought it was about time there was a book about us, so we asked our friend, Shirley Hughes, if she'd write one with different stories about our adventures. We wanted lots and lots of pictures and some strip cartoons too, because I like reading books with plenty of those. So she said she would, and here it is.

People like my mum and Jessie's mum are in it, of course, and Grandpa. And then, when Fred Laski and Winston and Spud Ellis, Becky, Big Joan and Little Joan and all that lot found out about there being this book about us, they had to go and shove in somehow like they always do. And we had to have my cat, Albert, in and Jessie's dog, Barkis, because they're very important. Then there's my baby sister, Gloria. We couldn't very well leave her out, worse luck.

I wanted there to be all sorts of exciting things like inter-galactic space-craft, man-eating robots and wild animals in this book. But, as Jessie says, there aren't any of those in our street, except for Albert (he's pretty wild sometimes). So it's just about US.

That's all, so now, get ready, here we are ...

Yours ~~sinseer~~
~~sinei~~
truly,

Chips and Jessie

X X

Don't forget us! woof, woof!

CONTENTS

TEA FOR TWO

Jessie wrote a letter to her friend, Chips:

Dear Chips

You are my very best frend. Please come to tea on Friday. It will be just the two of us.

luv
from Jessie Turner
xx

URGENT
hips Hall
Jtreet

Chips wrote back:

Meanwhile:

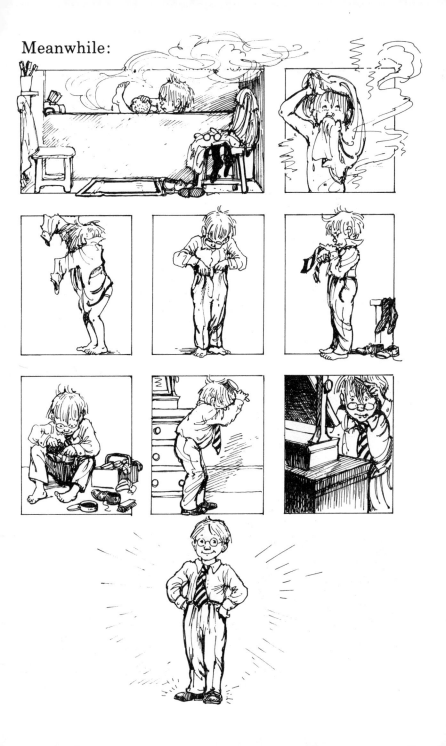

ANYBODY HERE
SEEN CHICO?

Chips and Jessie went to school together. They were in the same class as Fred Laski, Big Joan, Little Joan, Winston, Becky, Yasmin and Spud Ellis.

At school there lived a class hamster. His name was Chico.

Chico lived in a cage, in the passage, near to
where everyone hung up their coats. He had two
rooms in his cage, a bedroom where he buried
himself in sawdust and went to sleep, and a living-
room where he ran round and round on his wheel,
pedalling very fast with his little pink feet.

When Chico had eaten a meal,
his cheeks puffed out at the
sides, making him look very
fat. This was because he
kept his food in there
until he felt like
swallowing it.

One day their teacher, Mrs James, asked the class if anyone would offer to look after Chico during the half-term holiday. Chips was the first one to put up his hand. He liked Chico. He wanted to take him home and be able to get him out of his cage and play with him whenever he liked.

Mrs James said that if Chips was quite sure it would be all right, she would give him and Chico a lift home in her car after school on Friday. So it was all settled.

But when Chips told his mum, she didn't think having Chico was a good idea at all. A big argument started.

But you've got a cat already — surely that's enough?

It's only for a week, Mum!

We've got nowhere to put him!

I can have him in my bedroom.

Your BEDROOM! With all that sawdust and mess? You certainly can't keep him in there!

In the shed, then?

The cat might get in there and eat him. No, it's too much RESPONSIBILITY.

But I've told them at school I'm going to look after Chico. I can't go UN-telling them now!

You should have asked me first.

PLEASE, Mum!

Mum just wouldn't listen. She went off into the kitchen to bang saucepans about.

NO!

20

"People are always objecting and objecting and OBJECTING to the things I want to do!" Chips told Albert, the big tom cat. "You wouldn't eat Chico, would you, Albert?"

He'd be in a cage most of the time, so you'd jolly well have to leave him alone, see?

Albert closed his eyes to slits, and said nothing.

Then, luckily for Chips, Grandpa made a suggestion. He said that Chico's cage could go in the little store-room by the back door where the tools and washing-machine were kept. Chico would be safe there.

In the end Mum gave in.

Oh, all right, but you're not to keep letting him out, understood?

I'll look after him very well, really I will!

So Chips brought Chico home with him after all. The cage fitted nicely on to the shelf below the old paint tins.

I'm giving him lots to eat so he'll feel at home, Jessie.

Hmmm...

All that evening Chips kept popping in to make sure that Chico was feeling at home. He gave him some bits of cheese and a carrot and some food out of the special packet which Mrs James had left for him.

Jessie came round next morning to see how Chico was settling in. She thought Chips might be overfeeding him.

I had a couple of goldfish once who died because I overfed them!

They kept on opening and shutting their mouths and I thought they were hungry, so I gave them too many ants' eggs and they BOTH DIED!

Chico won't die, will he?

Chips was very anxious when he heard this. But Jessie added that she thought Chico probably wouldn't die, if Chips gave him only one bowlful of food a day. So Chips made up his mind to do as Jessie said, because she knew all about things like that. She belonged to a pet lovers' club and had a badge to prove it.

Chico was a big responsibility. For one thing, Albert was very interested in him. He kept sniffing at the store-room door. Once he even managed to get in there and climb up on to Chico's cage, but Chips found out and chased him off. Chips was very careful about keeping the door shut after that.

Chips' little sister, Gloria, was interested in Chico, too. She kept wanting to be held up to look inside his cage. But Chips wouldn't let her touch Chico.

One evening, when Gloria was safely in bed and Mum was getting supper ready, Chips opened the cage door and took Chico out. He held him in his hand and gently stroked the top of his head. He wanted to take him into the living-room, but he

was afraid that Albert might be about. Instead, in spite of what he'd been told, he secretly carried Chico up to his bedroom and quietly closed the door.

Chico was in a lively mood. He walked out of Chips' hand, right up his arm, over his shoulders and down the other arm. Chips could feel his little pink feet walking on the back of his neck. When he put Chico down on the floor he disappeared straight away under the chest-of-drawers. It was very difficult to get him out.

Next they had a lovely game of hide-and-seek in Chips' bed. Chico was very good at hiding. In the end Chips had to pull off all the sheets and blankets to find him.

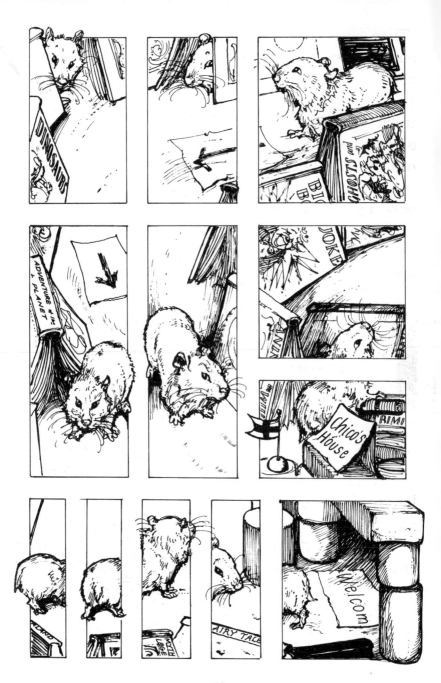

Then Chips arranged his books on the floor to make a little street for Chico to walk along. At the end of the street was a house made of toy bricks. Chips wanted Chico to walk along the street and into his house, but Chico had other ideas. He kept poking about, sniffing the books and wriggling his nose and whiskers.

Just then Chips heard Mum's voice calling from the bottom of the stairs.

CHIPS!

Your supper's ready!

He didn't know what to do about Chico. He couldn't take him back to his cage without Mum seeing him.

"Chips! Come along, your food's getting cold!" Mum called. She sounded cross. Chips was thinking very fast. There was nothing for it but to leave Chico in his bedroom. He would be quite safe in his street of books.

"Coming!" Chips shouted. He banged his bedroom door behind him and ran downstairs.

Oh help!

GULP!

Coming!

Supper seemed endless. Chips gobbled up his food as fast as he could. Afterwards he had to clear away the dishes, and then help Grandpa with the washing-up. At last he was free to run upstairs and rescue Chico.

When he reached the landing a terrible sight greeted him. His bedroom door stood slightly open, and there sat Albert!

Chips turned quite cold
with fright. He chased Albert
away and slammed the
bedroom door after him.
The books were all in place
except one. But Chico was
nowhere to be seen.

Chips started a frantic search. He pulled all the
things out of the cupboards and drawers, he shook
out the bedclothes, peered behind the furniture.

He even turned his shoes upside-down in case
Chico was hiding in one of them. But Chico had
gone. Perhaps by now he was *inside* Albert!

This was too much for Chips. He let out a loud
wail.

Mum came running upstairs to find out what was wrong.

You awful boy!

Whatever's the matter?

In between wails Chips had to tell her what he had done. And, of course, she was very angry.

I'm s-s-sorry!

You shouldn't have brought Chico upstairs when I PARTICULARLY told you not to!

NOW look what's happened!

I thought I'd shut the door, but Albert must have got in somehow and eaten Chico up!
Sob!

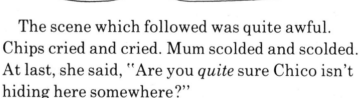

The scene which followed was quite awful. Chips cried and cried. Mum scolded and scolded. At last, she said, "Are you *quite* sure Chico isn't hiding here somewhere?"

Then they looked all over again in all the possible places. They searched every inch of the bedroom, the landing and the bathroom, but it was no use. So they went downstairs to look for Albert.

He was sitting in the hall with his tail tucked neatly round his paws. The tip of it was twitching gently.

You horrible cat!

"If you've eaten Chico, I'll never speak to you again, never!" shouted Chips. Albert looked pained and stalked off into the kitchen.

Then another terrible thought struck Chips. How was he going to tell them all at school what had happened to Chico?

Whatever will Mrs James and all the people at school say?

BOO HOO!

They all like Chico a lot. How am I going to tell them he's got eaten?

"He may turn up, I suppose," said Mum wearily. But that wasn't very comforting. In fact, Chips wasn't comforted at all. He wouldn't go to bed. He made such a fuss that he woke Gloria, who started to cry too. When Grandpa came in quite late, he found them all in the kitchen and a terrible commotion going on.

Grandpa sat down and smoked his pipe while they told him about it.

"This is difficult, very difficult indeed," he said. "You can't blame Albert. It's his nature. I don't have to tell you that it's your fault, Chips. You shouldn't have let Chico out and taken him upstairs when you were told not to. But you can't go back to school with an empty cage, that would never do."

"What *can* I do, then!" wailed Chips.

"If Chico doesn't turn up, we'll have to buy another one," said Grandpa firmly.

Chips stopped crying in astonishment.

When Grandpa told Chips to go off to bed, he did as he was told right away, for once. He even managed to get some sleep, in spite of worrying a lot about what had happened to Chico.

The next day Chips kept on asking Grandpa when they were going to buy another hamster, and Grandpa kept telling Chips that they had to wait a bit, just in case Chico was hiding somewhere, after all. But time went by and Chico did not appear. Chips began to get tearful again.

"We'll take the bus to Barrow Lane this afternoon, then," said Grandpa. So they did.

Jessie came with them to help carry Chico's cage. It was very difficult and bulky to hold on the crowded bus, but Grandpa said they were going to need it. He wasn't taking any chances over the new hamster escaping and getting lost.

Here we are!

At last they arrived at the pet shop. It was a lovely place. There were lots of hamsters, as well as mice, guinea-pigs, rabbits, kittens and goldfish, and a talking parrot who kept calling out cheeky things.

Chips and Jessie spent a long time looking at the hamsters. In the end Chips chose the one which looked most like Chico. They paid for him with Chips' pocket money. Then the shopkeeper helped them to put the new hamster into the cage and they all went home again on the bus.

"What are you going to call him?" Jessie
wanted to know.

Grandpa thought it would be a good idea to let
the children at school choose a name.

They'll enjoy thinking of
a name, and it will
make up for losing Chico.

Chips still dreaded going back to school. He
didn't know how he was going to explain to Mrs
James, Fred, Big Joan, Little Joan, Becky,
Winston, Yasmin and Spud Ellis and all the others
what had happened to Chico. But in the end, he
faced it bravely and told them everything. After it
was all over, he felt much better.

Well, er, you
see, it was
like this...

Mrs James suggested that everyone should write a name for the new hamster on a piece of paper. Then she would shake them all up in a box and pull one out, and that would be what they would call him. Chips wrote "KING KONG" on his piece of paper, but it didn't get pulled out of the box. Instead, the name "GOLDIE" was picked. Chips thought that was a pretty boring name, but he didn't mind much because he was so happy to have got through all the explaining.

So Goldie settled down in his cage at school and ran round and round on his wheel. Soon everyone got to like him just as much as they had liked Chico.

That evening Chips and Jessie were sitting on the kitchen table at Chips' house. Mum had taken Gloria to visit a friend and Grandpa was working in his garden shed. It was getting dark. Jessie was keeping Chips company by telling him all about a very spooky film she had seen on TV. It was about a man who had been locked up in a terrible prison on an island from which no one could escape, even though he'd done nothing wrong.

But, Jessie said, the man started to make a tunnel in the dungeon wall. He could only do it when the gaoler wasn't looking, so it took him a long time. He just had to keep on in the dark going *scratch, scratch, scratch* . . .

"Shh! what's that?" interrupted Chips. They both sat, silent. Over by the sink came a noise exactly like the one Jessie was describing — *scratch, scratch, scratch!*

Then the noise stopped. Nothing happened. Jessie started to go on with her story. The noise started again, a little louder.

"It's coming from just there, by the taps," said Chips.

They went over to look. Silence. They waited in the gathering dark. Before long they heard it — *scratch, scratch, scratch!*

Jessie was holding on to Chips very tightly. Something or somebody was coming through the wall! Chips was the first to guess who it was.

They put on the light. The scratching was getting louder and louder. Jessie rushed off to fetch Grandpa from the shed. A tiny crack was appearing in the wall, just over one of the taps. Grandpa took a good look.

"Perhaps it really is Chico," he said, and went off to find his small hammer and chisel.

He gently tapped a hole, and loosened the plaster round the pipes. They all waited.

Soon there was some more scratching, and some little bits of plaster fell down from inside the hole. Then a little face with bright eyes looked out at them.

Jessie and Chips fetched a newspaper and held it up to the hole for Chico to step out on to. But Chico took his time. He wanted to make the hole into a better shape. They had to wait while he nibbled away at the jagged bits of plaster and took them back into his tunnel, making them into a tidy heap.

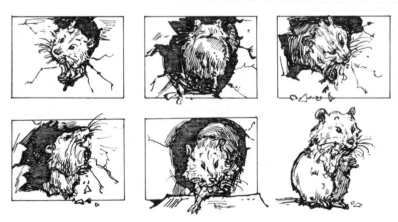

When the hole was just exactly as he wanted it, he stepped jauntily out on to the newspaper, and allowed himself to be lowered on to the draining-board, where he sat cleaning his whiskers.

"Just like the man in my story!" said Jessie.

Later, when they looked in the cupboard in Chips' bedroom, they found a tiny little hole in the floorboards. Chico had been under the floor all the time, and had climbed down the pipes inside the wall and ended up behind the kitchen sink.

The very next morning Chips took Chico back to school with him, safe in a cardboard box with holes in it for air. Everyone was *very* pleased to see him. Now there were two class hamsters. Luckily there was a spare cage for Chico to live in.

Mrs James said she thought that Chips might have wanted to keep Chico for himself. He had paid for Goldie out of his own money, after all. But Chips didn't want Chico at home any more.

"Too much RESPONSIBILITY," he said, remembering Mum's long word for it. "I think Albert ought to be the only pet in our house for a bit. And I'm going to be extra nice to him from now on, to make up for everything."

SHOPPING
AROUND

THE
BY-GONE FOX

Chips' mum had been asked to run a stall at the Church Bazaar on Saturday. Grandpa was going to look after Gloria, and Chips and Jessie were going to be helpers. They were going to sell By-Gones.

All week Mum collected up the By-Gones which people gave her for the stall. Chips didn't think much of them.

Before the Bazaar began Chips and Jessie were busy helping Mum arrange the stall. Quite a crowd of people were waiting to come in when the doors opened. Some of them stopped to look at the By-Gones. One or two of them even bought something.

Next to the By-Gones was a secondhand clothes stall. This was a big attraction. Winston's mum was doing a brisk trade. Winston was there, too, getting in her way.

Mrs Sharp, the school janitor's wife, arrived all dressed up in her fox fur, and made a bee-line for the secondhand clothes stall. She was an old enemy of Chips. She and her friend were looking for a bargain. Mrs Sharp couldn't make up her mind which coat suited her best. She thought she liked the blue one.

She took off her fur
and laid it over a chair.
Then she and her
friend became very
absorbed in discussing
whether or not the blue
coat fitted, while
Winston's mum made
encouraging remarks.

It's in lovely
condition — very
good value.

That colour
will go with
anything.

Yes, but is
it really ME?

Mrs Sharp turned this
way and that in front of
the mirror. She didn't
notice when somebody
moved her fur from the
chair and put it down
among the By-Gones.
Neither did anyone else.

I'm afraid Gloria's
in rather a bad
mood today.

Hello,
Grandpa!
We're
selling
LOTS of
By-Gones!

At this point Grandpa
appeared, pushing Gloria
in the buggy. Grandpa was
having a difficult afternoon.
Gloria was in one of her bad
moods. She sat in her
buggy, grizzling steadily.

When Gloria saw Mum she started to yell. She arched her back, kicked her legs about and tried to get out of her buggy.

I can't seem to do anything with her!

Oh, dear, it's her teeth again, I suppose.

Mama!

Can't you give her a drink or something?

I think you'll have to come with us and try to settle her down.

Waah!

So Mum and Grandpa took Gloria off in search of an orange-juice to cheer her up, and a cup of coffee for themselves. Chips and Jessie were left in charge of the By-Gones.

They had strict instructions to write down every sale while Mum was away. Jessie sold a cracked jug with a picture of swans on it. Chips tried very hard to sell an old clock.

It isn't going at the moment, but perhaps it will when you get it home...

You could always stick on another minute hand.

A young lady was hovering round the stall, idly picking over the things. Her eye fell on Mrs Sharp's fox fur.

When she asked the price, Chips promptly told her two pounds. It was the first sum which came into his head.

The young lady put the fur over her shoulder with the head and front paws hanging down the front, looking very foxy indeed. She stroked the fur. Luckily she was hardly listening to Chips' eager sales-talk.

"I think I'll take it," said the young lady. She handed Chips two pound notes from her purse and went off into the crowd with the fox fur draped over her shoulder. Chips was very pleased with himself.

Mrs Sharp had by this time tried on five different coats and decided against them all. She turned round to collect her fur and found it had gone! She was not the sort of person to avoid making a fuss. What was more, she had a very loud voice.

She set up a great hue and cry, saying that her fur had been stolen. Chips turned scarlet in the face when he realized what had happened. He looked round desperately for the young lady, but she seemed to have disappeared completely.

Chips plunged into the crowd, leaving Jessie to look after the By-Gones. Mrs Sharp walked off in a rage. She and her friend were going to ask the Vicar to make an announcement on his loudspeaker.

Things looked bad. But fortunately, at that very moment, Jessie looked up and saw the young lady. She had come to ask for her money back! She had decided that she didn't much like wearing a fur with paws and a foxy face, after all.

Jessie was delighted. She quickly gave the young lady her two pounds back. Then she called out to Chips, holding the fur high above her head in triumph. Chips was so relieved that he rushed up and started to dance a foxtrot with it round the By-Gones stall. But Jessie seized it from him and hurried off.

She was just in time to return it to Mrs Sharp before the Vicar made his announcement.

"Where did you find it, then?" Mrs Sharp asked Jessie, suspiciously. Her eyes were as beady as the ones on her fox fur. Jessie explained that it had been put on the By-Gones stall by mistake.

Mrs Sharp whisked her fur round her neck and went off, very huffily, with her friend. The Vicar was pleased. He told Jessie that she had saved the afternoon. He said that she and Chips and Winston had done so well that they could finish up all that was left on the home-made cake and sweet stall when the Bazaar was over. Which wasn't a bad ending to a foxy tale.